NOTHING
IS
STRANGE

Mike Russell

ISBN-10:1502901080

ISBN-13:978-1502901088

www.strangebooks.com

Contents

NOTHING
IS
STRANGE

Cream Tea

Mr Spencer's scones are legendary. Their ingredients are mixed in such perfect harmony that eating them obliterates all the obstacles to love that exist within one's soul.

Impeccably dressed as ever, in his dark blue suit and yellow cravat, Mr Spencer stands behind the counter of 'Mr Spencer's Tea Rooms' with a serene expression upon his face.

Mr Spencer's only customers are a young man and a young woman who are sat by the window, sipping from cups of tea. They are not eating scones. They do not like scones.

Suddenly the young man picks up a teaspoon, reaches across the table and drops it down the front of the woman's shirt.

Behind the counter, a fountain of tiny, white lights erupts from a small, round hole in the top of Mr Spencer's head.

The young woman picks up a bowl of sugar lumps and tips it into the man's lap.

The fountain of lights issuing from the hole in Mr Spencer's head grows a little higher.

The young man throws the remains of his tea at the woman's face.

The fountain of lights grows higher still.

The young woman picks up her empty teacup. She is about to hurl it at the young man when Mr Spencer calmly steps out from behind the counter, walks over to the couple, points at the fountain issuing from his head and politely asks:

'Can you see this?'

The couple turn and scowl at Mr Spencer, angry at his interruption of their escalating violence. They look at the fountain then, in unison, shrug and say:

'Yes.'

'Do you know what it is?' asks Mr Spencer.

'No,' they say in unison.

'Then please allow me to show you,' Mr Spencer says and opens his mouth wide.

The couple peer into Mr Spencer's mouth and are surprised to see darkness dotted with tiny, white lights.

Mr Spencer reaches his hands into his trouser pockets, produces two small telescopes and hands them to the couple.

'Look closer,' he says.

The couple extend the telescopes, point them into Mr Spencer's mouth and look through them.

'I can see the Earth!' the couple say in unison.

'Look closer,' Mr Spencer says.

'I can see this building!' the couple say in unison.

'Look closer,' Mr Spencer says.

'I can see myself!' the couple say in unison.

Then, whilst still looking through the telescopes, the couple wave out of the window at themselves.

Mr Spencer closes his mouth. The stars continue to issue forth from the hole in the top of his head, shooting up into the air, fading as they fall, then dying upon the floor.

'Now,' Mr Spencer says, '*please* have a scone.'

The Diaries of Sun City

Dear Diary,

Hello. It is Monday. I live in Sun City. Sun City is a city that is entirely contained inside an enormous concrete building in the shape of a sun. Its rays house our living quarters; its circular centre is where we work and shop. No one has ever been outside of the city; it is generally suspected that the environment outside of the city is uninhabitable.

People write diaries for a particular reason here, where our social etiquette is constricting. Diaries are so popular that they have their own shop. The shop is called 'We Are Diaries'. I have not owned a diary until now. The idea of placing my most secret, most sacred feelings out in the world terrifies me but today I bought a small, black book with blank, white pages and the word 'Diary' embossed on its cover.

I walked from the shop and through the city centre with the diary in my pocket and caught the bus that runs up and down the concrete ray that houses my apartment. My apartment is at the very end of the concrete ray.

Inside my apartment, I sat facing the far wall. I lay the diary on my lap, opened it at the first page, then began to write in it with pen and ink.

Why can I not tell Miss Baraclough that I care for her? It would be wrong to of course, inappropriate. She would be offended, that would be expected of her.

Reluctantly, her associates would be obliged to sever their relations with me; my associates would be informed and forced to sever their relations with me also. I would feel ashamed because it would be expected of me. Yet I would not feel ashamed when talking to you dear Diary; I would be proud. But I cannot say it to her so this ink is wasted.

Dear Diary,

It is Tuesday. Despite my dismissal of its worth, I have decided to write to you again. When I opened the diary this evening I discovered the first page to be blank! My memory of writing on the page is clear. Is my memory lying to me?

Dear Diary,

It is Wednesday. When I opened the diary this evening the first page was blank again. Is the ink fading? I am scared. Imagine saying that to a colleague. 'Mr Barton, I am scared.' Imagine his horror, his embarrassment, his contempt. Tomorrow, I will whisper it to his back.

Dear Diary,

It is Thursday. When I opened the diary this evening, the first page was blank again. I decided to count the pages. I counted 362. The pages are disappearing. Someone must be stealing the pages. I have begun constructing elaborate scenarios from my suspicions. Who would want to know my secret thoughts? But had I not once wished to see inside Miss Baraclough's diary? If I had spied it when visiting her in her apartment and she had briefly left the room to make a cup of tea, would I not have been tempted to steal a glance at a few words? From this confession, dear Diary, I deduce that the pages could have been stolen by absolutely anyone.

I expect that by tomorrow evening this page will also have disappeared.

Dear Diary,

It is Friday. I was right; the page has gone. Today, on the bus, I wanted to shout obscenities and bare myself to the other passengers. My confessions to you, dear Diary, are becoming more honest with the thought that they are being read. I am no longer scared of my words being seen because they are evidently being read by someone who welcomes them, who needs them. But I am fantasising. My door is bolted from the inside at night and there are no windows in my apartment. How then are the pages disappearing? Am I destroying them myself in my sleep? Is there a part of me that abhors these words, that would rather I was a perfect citizen with no feelings that need to be hidden? I will stay at Miss Baraclough's tonight.

Dear Diary,

It is Saturday. The page has gone. The 'We Are Diaries' shop is wrong; they are not diaries. I do not write to them and it is not this book that I am writing to either. I am not addressing these paper pages or their cardboard cover. Dear Diary, who are you?

Dear Diary,

It is Sunday. I want to leave the city. What is outside of the city? Is that where you reside? Do you have a throne on the other side of the world?

Dear Diary,

It is Monday. I am hammering a chisel into the far wall of my apartment, the end of the concrete ray. Bang follows bang with no lessening of passion. My desire grows as my energy fades. Bang. Bang. It falls away in chunks.

I can see a little light that grows.

The hole is big enough to crawl through.

I crawl through.

It is so bright! The ground is covered in pages, knee deep, for as far as I can see. White pages covered in writing in different hands lay naked, exposed, pressed against one another. It is overwhelming. I wade through them.

I walk in a straight line all day, bewildered but purposeful, towards Diary's throne.

In the distance I can see other people. They are also wading through the pages, striding from every direction towards the same destination, fearless, with nothing to lose. Could it be that everyone has broken through their respective concrete rays at the same time and for the same reason as I?

When we reach a distance where Diary's throne should be in sight, we all realise that it is not there, and that it is not the throne that we are walking towards but each other.

The air is full of unrestricted speech.

We now no longer live inside the sun but are illuminated by it.

Now we become the throne.

Now we are Diary.

Dunce

Everyone calls Dunce 'Dunce'. Everyone thinks that Dunce is an idiot. I used to think so too but not any more.

Dunce is completely bald and has a really pointed head so the temptation to get him paralytic on his thirtieth birthday, carry him to the tattooist's and get a nice big 'D' smack bang in the middle of his forehead was too much for me. Trouble is he can't afford to have it removed so he wears a big plaster over it. Gangs of children tease him.

'What's underneath the plaster, mister? Show us!'

They swear he has a third eye under there.

My name is Bill but Dunce calls me 'Fez' on account of my hat. I've known Dunce for over sixteen years. I don't have to use my memory to work that out; I just count the number of boxes of Turkish Delight I've got stashed in my cupboard. Dunce buys me a box every birthday. Dunce thinks that because I wear a fez I must be Turkish (I'm not) and that being Turkish I must like that powder-covered gunk (I don't, I hate the stuff).

On my last birthday, after saying:

'No, Dunce, I'll eat it later,' and stashing box number sixteen in the cupboard, I decided to take Dunce to the theatre. He'd never been before.

The play was called 'Death in the Dark'. We had front row seats. Dunce was captivated. He stared at the actors with a gaping mouth.

The lights dimmed to darkness. Kitty Malone, the beautiful star of the show, was stood centre stage. A shot was heard. Dunce jumped right out of his seat.

'What was that?' he said.

The lights came back on and Kitty was lying in a pool of blood. Dunce let out a scream then shouted:

'Someone call for an ambulance! And the police!'

The audience thought that Dunce was an actor, that the play was being cleverly extended beyond the stage, questioning the boundaries of theatre.

'What's wrong with you?' Dunce shouted at the audience. 'How can you carry on as if nothing has happened?'

'This is wonderful, just wonderful,' I heard someone say behind me.

Kitty was stoically sticking to her role, thinking that the show must go on, but Dunce was clambering up onto the stage, crying, stroking Kitty's hair and checking her pulse.

'She's alive!' he shouted with relief.

'No I'm not!' Kitty hissed at him through clenched teeth.

That was it; I was in hysterics. What a birthday treat

this was turning out to be.

'I'm acting. It's part of the play. No one really shot me,' Kitty hissed at Dunce.

The realisation was excruciatingly slow. I watched Dunce's face change from shock to confusion to understanding to embarrassment. He made his way back to his seat. He didn't speak or look at me until the play was over. The play got a standing ovation and we headed for the bar.

Kitty was in the bar too. She smiled at Dunce who blushed. She seemed to be fascinated by the top of his head. She walked over and invited him to her dressing room.

Twelve hours later and Dunce was in love! How about that? And what's more, Kitty was in love too! And not only that but they were in love with each other! Kitty fell for Dunce. Not 'fell for' as in 'was deceived by' because there's no deception where Dunce is concerned, he can't do it, but she fell from her deceptions towards him. I couldn't believe it.

'It won't last,' I said to Dunce. 'Enjoy it while you can but face facts: you are Dunce and she is Kitty Malone. Think about it.'

Dunce told me that Kitty had a thing about ice cream cones, a fetish you could say. She ate six a day. She liked to bite off the tip of the cone and suck out all the ice cream. She had a recording of ice cream van music that she played whilst they were having sex. She was forever stroking the top of Dunce's head.

Then came the day. Dunce came round looking really worried.

'Fez, have you seen Kitty? Do you know where she is?'

'No, I haven't seen her. Why? What's the problem?'

'I had a dream last night,' Dunce said. 'I dreamt that I was in bed and I looked at the calendar by the side of my bed and it was tonight. I put out my hand to touch Kitty but she wasn't there. There was just this cold sludge covering her side of the bed and this smell: vanilla. It was melted ice cream.'

'So what's the problem?'

'I think that something is going to happen to Kitty. I have to find her before tonight. I don't want to wake up tomorrow morning alone in a bed full of melted ice cream.'

'Dunce, dreams don't mean anything and prophecies are impossible. Sit yourself down. Let's have a couple of beers.'

I opened a cupboard, reached in to get the beers and a

28

pile of boxes of Turkish Delight toppled over and fell out, breaking open and spilling their contents all over the floor. Dunce looked at the boxes then looked at me. I watched his face go through the same slow transformation from shock to confusion to understanding to embarrassment that I had witnessed so many times before.

'You don't like Turkish Delight?' he said.

I said nothing and guiltily handed him a beer.

Dunce sighed then said:

'So why did I have that dream?'

'No reason at all,' I said.

We sat in silence for a while then Dunce suddenly stood up.

'It's no good, Fez, I have to find her.'

Dunce found Kitty in the centre of town, lying on the pavement in a pool of blood. An ambulance and the police were on their way. An ice cream vendor was crying and yelling:

'I don't understand! I don't understand!'

A huge, plastic ice cream cone was protruding from Kitty's chest. It had fallen from on top of the ice cream shop for no apparent reason, smashed through her rib cage and crushed her heart.

Dunce cried. Then he cried some more. The next day,

he cried and the day after that he cried. Three weeks later, he awoke, dressed, ate some breakfast, then cried. The next day, he came round to see me. He was crying.

'Hello Dunce,' I said. 'Do you want a beer?'

'What's wrong with you?' he said. 'How can you carry on as if nothing has happened?'

'It was an accident, Dunce,' I said angrily, 'a random occurrence. These things happen. You just have to get on with life. Why are you so stupid?'

I regretted saying it as soon as I heard it come out of my mouth. Dunce stared at me with tears in his eyes.

'A fez is only a severed cone,' Dunce said. 'At least I have a point.'

I took off my hat and looked at it sullenly. Dunce had a point that he had a point. If he'd found Kitty a moment earlier... if I hadn't delayed him with my arrogance, my cynicism...

'Fez,' Dunce said, 'you remember the tears that I cried in the theatre when I thought that Kitty was dead but she wasn't? I think that the tears I am crying now are the same as those. I didn't understand what was going on in the theatre and I didn't understand what was going on when the cone fell on her. I think that maybe we only cry because we don't understand what is going on. Maybe if we understood what is really going on we wouldn't cry at all, ever.'

Dunce smiled through his tears and beneath the plaster on his forehead I swear I saw something move.

The Warehouse

Daphne and Sylvester want to prove that their love is real. They want to prove that their love is real to the whole world. That is why they are currently having sexual intercourse in the middle of their local shopping centre on a Saturday afternoon.

The shoppers turn and stare in disbelief.

'Look at us!' Daphne and Sylvester call out between heavy breaths. 'We love each other!'

'You're deceiving each other!' someone shouts at them.

'You're deceiving yourselves!' someone else shouts at them.

Someone calls the police.

It is night. Daphne and Sylvester are asleep in their bed. The doorbell rings. The couple awake. They do not argue about who is going to answer the door, no, Daphne and Sylvester both get up, both put on their matching dressing gowns, then both walk downstairs and open the door together.

Standing on the doorstep is the policeman who arrested them the previous day. But he is not wearing his police uniform; he is wearing pyjamas. And although his eyes are open, he is snoring.

'Hello,' say Daphne and Sylvester.

The policeman looks at them with a vacant expression then says:

'Everything that is not a thing is a thing in The Warehouse.'

Then he falls to his knees and starts drawing a diagram with his finger in the dust on the doorstep.

Daphne and Sylvester exchange a look of bewilderment. Sylvester walks back upstairs, then returns with a camera and photographs the policeman. Oblivious, the officer continues with his drawing until he deems it complete, then he stands, turns around and, still snoring, wanders away.

Sylvester photographs the completed drawing, then says:

'Well, these photographs should persuade the police to drop their charges.'

'If only we could photograph our love,' says Daphne, 'then I wouldn't care if they charged us.'

The following morning, Sylvester exclaims:

'It's a map! It's a map of the town!'

He hands the photograph of the policeman's drawing to Daphne.

'So it is,' she says. 'Is that our house?' she asks, pointing.

'Yes, I think so. But that line leading from it doesn't make any sense. It seems to pass right through buildings.'

'What is that place that it leads to?'

'I don't know. Maybe it isn't a map.'

It is the day of Daphne and Sylvester's court appearance and they are getting ready to leave their house. Both are dressed in their smartest clothes.

'I'm ready,' says Daphne.

'I don't want to go,' Sylvester says.

'But I thought you were looking forward to showing them the photographs,' Daphne says.

'Let's follow the map instead and see where it takes us,' says Sylvester.

'But we're not even sure that it is a map.'

'So what? Let's follow it anyway.'

Daphne laughs. She is suddenly excited at the prospect.

'I love you, Sylvester.'

'I love you, Daphne.'

With the photograph of the policeman's drawing held between them, Daphne and Sylvester leave their house and walk wherever the line on the map takes them.

As soon as they start to follow the map, their surroundings begin to change. The map contradicts what Daphne and Sylvester know of the town: streets run counter to streets; buildings are in place of buildings... With every step they take along the map's route, their environment changes to match it. Even the sky looks different; it appears to be neither day nor night.

'Where is everyone?' Daphne asks. 'The town is deserted!'

The map leads Daphne and Sylvester to the place where the courthouse should be but the courthouse is not there. They stand looking at the empty space between the houses in bemused wonder. The map then leads them through the empty space, the walls of which narrow to an alleyway.

They emerge from the alleyway and find themselves standing outside a huge warehouse. They try the door. It is open. They tiptoe inside.

Daphne and Sylvester are in an enormous room full of filing cabinets. They choose one of the filing cabinets at random, then choose one of its drawers at random and open it. It is full of file-cards. They choose one of the file-cards at random, pull it out and read it:

'Daphne and Sylvester.'

They stare at one another. They look through the other cards to check that they are not all identical. They are not. Each card is printed with a pair of different names and on the back of each card is a unique number.

The number on the back of Daphne and Sylvester's card is:

'492713586.'

Daphne and Sylvester exchange a glance, then close the drawer. They look at the map, then follow it through the room to a door in the far wall. They open the door and emerge into another enormous room. This room is full of shelves stacked with cardboard boxes. Each box is numbered. Daphne and Sylvester search for the number on their file card. Eventually, they find it. Between them, they manage to lift the box down from its shelf and carry it back through the room of filing cabinets and out of the building. They carry the box back through the space between the houses where the courthouse should be, back through the unfamiliar streets and towards their house. Before going inside, they look up at the sky. It is still neither night nor day. They carry the box inside their house.

Inside, their home is just as it was. They walk upstairs, enter their bedroom, then place the cardboard box in the middle of their bed. Now they kneel on the bed opposite one another, with the cardboard box between them.

'What if it is empty?' Sylvester asks.

'Then we part,' Daphne says.

Together, with their breath held, Daphne and Sylvester open the lid of the box, then peer inside. Euphoria engulfs them. They reach inside the box, then lift out its contents and sit it on the bed between them. They grin and laugh and hug and kiss.

Between them, on the bed, is their love. It is beautiful, colourful, soft in places, hard in others, glowing, pulsating, tentacles waving, petals and wings opening. They touch it, feeling its cavities and protrusions. A perfume emanates from it, both strange and intoxicating. It makes a sound like music. They cuddle it and stroke it and fondle it and kiss it.

Daphne and Sylvester now carefully lift their love up between them and stand in front of the window. They look out of the window, hold their love aloft and smile. Down in the street is stood everyone else in the world, who all look up at them and cheer.

The Miracle

Imagine a girl. Imagine a car. Imagine how the two might combine. The girl could be inside the car in various positions or on top of the car like in an advertisement. Or the two could be sliced and shuffled together, minced, mangled, mixed. The combinations are numerous. Imagine what the girl could do to the car. Imagine what the car could do to the girl. Some of these imaginings might seem shocking or unpleasant but feelings aren't real are they?

A little, blonde girl called Sandy Grace is playing with a doll and a toy car on a yellow carpet. Sandy grins as she stands the doll on the carpet, then pushes the car towards the doll. The doll has been printed with a fixed grin. It continues to grin, as does Sandy as she hits the doll with the car. Sandy happily bashes the car against the doll again and again until the doll breaks.

Sandy's mother, Sandra Grace, has been watching her daughter with indifference.

Sandra Grace is crossing a road. She is carrying a bag over her shoulder. Suddenly a car races towards her, strikes her, then continues on its way without stopping or even slowing. Sandra lies dead on the road. Her bag has split open, revealing a white robe that the wind is now blowing, billowing across the street.

The body remains where it is until another car races towards it and is unable to drive over the obstacle, however much the driver tries. The driver stops his car, curses that he is now late for work, then calls the police on his mobile phone.

The police officer who eventually arrives at the scene is called Geoff. Geoff walks over to the body, gives it a kick then says:

'There goes my early night, bitch.'

Desmond Grace is sat in his office, staring at a sheet of paper printed with numbers that is lying in front of him on his desk. There is a knock at the door.

'Who is it?' shouts Desmond, irritably.

The door opens and Geoff, the police officer, enters the room.

'Mr Grace?' Geoff asks.

'Yes?'

'Your daughter is dead.'

Geoff is renowned for his economy of language, his unwavering adherence to the facts, so much so that rumours of promotion have been circling him for some time.

'Oh fucking hell!' shouts Desmond. 'It's just one thing after another. I'm never going to finish reading these numbers. How did she die?'

'She was knocked down by a car.'

'I'm not surprised,' says Desmond. 'She was always day-dreaming.'

'You are required to identify the body as soon as possible.'

'Oh for fuck's sake. Right, come on then.'

Desmond stands up to leave but the telephone on his desk rings. He picks it up.

'Yes?' he snaps.

'Hello Mr Grace. Do you know where Sandra is? There is no answer at her house.'

'She's dead.'

'Oh, I see. That would explain it. Thank you. Goodbye.'

Desmond slams the receiver down then the two men leave the office.

In an underground room, a man dressed in a white robe puts down his telephone receiver. He is the High Priest of The House of the Human Clouds. He turns to face a number of similarly dressed people and says:

'Sandra is dead.'

The men and women look at each other with blank expressions.

'We must contemplate her death,' the High Priest says.

'Perhaps Sandra is our saviour.'

The brothers and sisters of The House of the Human Clouds stand in a circle around the High Priest and hold hands. From a pocket inside his robe, the High Priest produces a glass bottle and a cork. The brothers and sisters all think about Sandra and they think about her death. Each of them concentrates.

The High Priest approaches one of the members of the circle and holds the glass bottle under one of her eyes. The High Priest stares hard into that eye, searching for just a single drop of liquid, but finds nothing. He moves the bottle to beneath the woman's other eye. His other hand holds the cork, poised, ready to trap the sacred prize, but again there is nothing. He moves slowly around the inside of the circle, from eye to eye. The bottle remains empty.

In the mortuary, Desmond and Geoff look at Sandra's corpse.

'Yes, that is my daughter,' Desmond says.

Then he looks closer at his daughter's face and suddenly feels... odd.

'I am leaving now,' Desmond says to Geoff. 'I am a busy man.'

Then he strides out of the building.

As Desmond walks down the street, he thinks that he must be ill. The odd feeling is growing and he has to

43

stand still. It is overwhelming. He looks at the people passing by and actually considers stopping one of them and asking for help. The feeling continues to grow and now it is changing him. His mouth is curling down at the corners and his brows are frowning. He struggles against it.

'Is this death?' Desmond thinks.

His pulse races, he sweats. Thoughts of Sandra fill his mind: useless, irrational thoughts. Something begins to well up in his eyes. He blinks.

'Are my eyes bleeding?' he thinks.

He touches the liquid that is now running down his cheeks. He looks at his hand. The liquid is transparent.

'What is happening to me?' he thinks.

He tries to speak but only makes tiny yelps and little moans. He stands motionless, helpless.

A substantial gathering has formed in front of him. All are watching his face, in wonder. A number of people dressed in white robes approach. One of them rushes forward with a glass bottle and a cork; the others lay flower wreaths at Desmond's feet.

The morning paper shows a photograph of Desmond's contorted and dripping face. The headline reads:

'Person Cries!'

The text beneath the photograph reads:

'A man was found yesterday evening, standing in Main Street, with what appeared to be tears pouring from his eyes. Medical examinations have found no cause for the secretion. The House of the Human Clouds has claimed the occurrence to be a miracle. Experts suspect that the whole episode is simply an elaborate hoax.'

The Meeting

Two detached houses stand side by side. One is painted red and one is painted blue. A white stone path leads from the door of each house. The two paths meet twenty-five metres from the doors and become one. This single path continues for fifty metres then divides into two again. These two paths both continue for another twenty-five metres, then stop at two doors of two different buildings, one painted red and one painted blue. These two buildings are different from the two houses. The houses have pointed roofs and windows front and back; the other two buildings are half as high with flat roofs and no windows. The red house is opposite the red building; the blue house is opposite the blue building.

Apart from these four buildings and the paths between them, there is nothing but grass, neatly mown, as far as I can see. It has always been like this.

I am a man. I live in the red house. I have always lived there. The house is well furnished. In exchange for these comforts I work in the red building.

The red building contains a single room, which is painted the same red as the building's exterior. Inside, I stand upon two black silhouettes of feet printed on the floor. In front of me, in the centre of the room, is a red plinth. On top of the plinth, in its centre, is a round, red button. On the far wall is a dial. It is this dial that I watch, with my hand hovering above the button. The hand of the dial turns. At the top of the dial is a small, red arrow that points down. When the dial's hand points at the arrow, I press the button. The hand continues to turn until it points at the arrow again, then I press the button again. Round and round, the hand of the dial turns. Life goes by.

Life is fine... except that every morning I awake with a pain in the centre of my forehead. The pain makes it difficult for me to raise my head, so that when I am standing I am forced to stare at the ground. As the day progresses, the pain fades but the next morning it returns just as before.

When the hand of the dial stops turning, it is time to go home. Then I leave the red building and walk along the path towards the red house. It is then that I see her, walking towards me along the path. We pass each other every evening. I have never seen her face. Whenever I see her, she is looking at the ground, her head hanging down. We pass each other every morning too but then of course it is *my* head that hangs because of the pain. It is almost certain that she lives in the blue house and it is almost certain that she works in the blue building. She almost certainly works nights. Her face is a mystery to me. It is a blur in a sharply focused world.

It is morning. I awake with the pain in the centre of my forehead as usual and walk to work. My head hangs. I hear her footsteps. I hear them grow louder. Something has been wrong for a long time. Something has been missing from my world. There are questions that have never been asked. I cannot explain but there are questions that are growing, that are becoming stronger than the pain in my forehead. My neck is slowly straightening. I want to see her face. Is it possible that she only hangs her head in the evenings? I push through the pain. Her head is not hanging. I see her face. How can I describe it? A list of observations would be profoundly insufficient. It is better to say that seeing her face renders the rest of the world indistinct.

'Morning,' she says.

'Morning,' I say. 'I expected you to say *evening*. You work nights don't you? In the blue building?'

'Yes. My evenings are your mornings. I am on my way home.'

'You always hang your head in the evenings, my evenings, your mornings.'

'Yes. I suffer from headaches every morning,' she says.

'I always awake with a pain just here,' she points at the centre of her forehead.

'Oh,' I say. 'Well, I must get to work. See you.'

'See you.'

How different everything now seems.

The hand of the dial turns. I press the button. The hand of the dial turns. I press the button...

The dial stops turning. I leave the red building and walk home. I see her walking towards me. Her head is hanging but, as we reach each other, she slowly straightens her neck, pushing through her pain, and looks at me. Knowing that pain, I reach out and gently touch her shoulder.

'I know what causes my headaches,' she says.

I am shocked. I have never before thought that such a question could be asked. What causes the pain? I stare at her in anticipation.

'I didn't sleep last night,' she says, 'because... I was thinking about you.'

I flush in embarrassment.

'I was lying face up on my bed,' she continues, 'with my eyes open, when suddenly a small trap-door opened in the ceiling. I was so scared that I couldn't move. Then a small, red hammer emerged on the end of a red rod. It stopped just above my head, then hit me in the centre of my forehead.'

I stare at her, stunned.

'A few moments went by, then it hit me again. The hammer hit my forehead at regular intervals all through the night. Then it retreated back into the ceiling and the trap-door closed. I can't talk anymore or I'll be late for work. I'm going to sleep on the floor tonight. See you.'

It is evening. I am at home. I walk into my bedroom, stand on my bed and examine the ceiling. I find nothing to confirm or disprove my suspicions, so I lay down and fall asleep.

It is morning and I awake without any pain. It is extraordinary. It has never happened before. Something is definitely happening. I leave the house and walk to work with my head up. I see her walking towards me. She looks frightened. Before I can speak, she says:
'I have something to tell you. I have been thinking about my job...'
'What is it that you do?'
'I press a blue button. But I never before considered what it might do. Isn't that insane? I just never thought that the question could be asked...'
What does the button do? Why have I never asked that question? My life is being opened up. I am terrified.
'What does the button do?' I ask.
'The blue button is on top of a blue plinth. Behind the plinth is a trap-door set into the floor. Today, instead of pressing the button, I lifted the trap-door. It revealed steps descending into darkness. I climbed down the

steps. When I reached the bottom, a light came on. I was in a room the same size as the one above. A blue rod was protruding from the ceiling, emerging from the underside of the plinth and descending to the floor. The rod bent at ninety degrees, travelled along the floor, then disappeared into a hole in the wall. The hole was just big enough to crawl into. I followed the rod through a long tunnel until I eventually came up against a wall. There, the rod bent at ninety degrees again and travelled up through a hole in the ceiling. There was a ladder that led up into the hole, which I climbed. The rod bent at ninety degrees again and I crawled through a horizontal tunnel until the rod came to an end above a trap-door in the floor. The end of the rod was attached to a small, blue hammer. I opened the trap door and looked through.'

'What did you see?' I ask.

She draws breath.

'I saw a man asleep in bed,' she says. Then she quickly adds, 'It was too dark to see his face. It could have been anyone.'

'So,' I say, 'there is someone out there who wakes up every morning with a pain in the middle of their forehead just like you and I bet they press a red button every day at work.'

'Yes.'

I cast around for words but remain silent. Then she says:

'Will you kiss me please?'

Barry and the Triplets

'You are listening to Radio Noise and this is Loud Eric's Pop Ascension where we are about to reach the Zenith. That's the week's most popular recording, for those of you new to the show. And it's a special week here at Loud Eric's Pop Ascension because the most popular recording this week also happens to be the most popular recording ever! That's right noise-listeners, the recording that you've been listening to the most over the last seven days has outsold every other recording that has ever been made. So who is it that has reached this extraordinary position? You know the answer. It's those three lovely ladies known only as... The Triplets. But before we play their recording let's remind ourselves of this unique group's lowly beginnings by hearing the story of their rise to fame straight from the mouth of the man who discovered them. Yes, you heard right, exclusive to Radio Noise, speaking to us live from his prison cell, it's Barry Hambury!... Hello Barry.'

'Hello Eric. Thanks for having me on the show. I'm really pleased to be speaking to you.'

'I'm sure you are, Barry. After a week in solitary confinement I guess you'd be happy to speak to anyone.'

'That's a fair point, Eric.'

'So Barry, tell us about the day that you discovered the most popular recording artists of all time, the day that you discovered The Triplets.'

'Well Eric, I was walking through town, not far from this prison in fact, when I heard a strange sound coming from a dustbin.'

'What sort of sound, Barry?'

'It was three voices, Eric. Two of them sounded terrible... hideous, wailing screeches... but one of them, one of those three voices, was the most beautiful sound I'd ever heard.'

'Can you describe it to us, Barry?'

'It was high, it was soft, and it was sweet. It was just beautiful, Eric, just beautiful.'

'It was beautiful was it, Barry?'

'It was beautiful, Eric.'

'So what did you do, Barry?'

'I walked towards that dustbin, Eric... I was drawn towards it by that beautiful sound... and I lifted the lid.'

'Do you want to tell our listeners what you saw inside that bin, Barry?'

'I sure do, Eric. I saw three babies in that bin, three baby girls.'

'Damn. What was your first thought, Barry?'

'I'm sorry to say this, Eric, but my first thought was me.'

'What do you mean, Barry?'

'I mean that those babies looked like a gift to me, Eric...

and a gift they turned out to be... but not in the way that I was hoping for... I saw them and I thought I'd found the answer to all my problems but it was an answer that was hidden from me.'

'What do you mean, Barry?'

'One of those babies was destined for the stage. That beautiful voice was going to make me a million. That was my first thought. But which baby was it? You see, the moment I lifted that dustbin lid, Eric, those three babies went quiet. When I looked inside, not one of them was making any noise. But I figured sooner or later they'd make their sounds again. All I had to do was wait. Then I'd snatch the good one and life would start to get better.'

'So you planned to leave the other two to die, Barry?'

'I'm sorry to say that I did, Eric. See, I thought, hey, I wasn't the one that had left them there in the first place... and there was no way I could afford to look after all three, so by taking one I'd be doing a good thing... and it stood to reason, I thought, that I should take the one that was going to be able to pay its way... and if I benefited from that then, well, that was what I deserved for saving it. I'm not trying to justify it, Eric. I know I was wrong. I just want your listeners to understand how it was.'

'I appreciate that, Barry.'

'So I waited. I stood looking at those three babies and I waited... and I waited... and I waited... nothing. Not a sound. I waited for hours until I figured that those baby girls weren't going to make no noise ever again and I... I'm sorry to say it but I picked up that dustbin lid and I put it back on that dustbin, ready to walk away, thinking that if they were no use to me then I didn't want them. But the moment I fitted that lid back on, the voices started again: the two wailing screeches and the one sweet sound... so I seized my chance, I picked that lid up fast. But as soon as I looked inside the bin, the babies went quiet again. It was spooky, Eric. It was like they knew what I was planning... it was like they knew!'

'Hmmm...'

'So I figured I'd take all three home. I figured I'd take them home and watch them until they revealed who was who. So I put the lid back on the bin, ready to carry it home, and damn it if they didn't start their noise again! I carried that bin home, with those three voices echoing inside it, then when I was inside my house I opened the bin and they stopped. I was beginning to hate them, Eric, I felt like they were toying with me, you know? I put the babies in my spare room and watched them for the rest of the day. Nothing. Not a sound. Occasionally I'd close my eyes, to fool them that I'd fallen asleep, and they'd start their noise... then I'd open my eyes real quick. But as soon as my eyes were open they'd go silent. It was infuriating, Eric, infuriating! The next day I went out and bought a CCTV security system and set it up in their room. I left them there alone with the camera pointing at them, then went and sat in the park. When I returned home, I rewound the footage and sat myself down in front of the monitor, all comfy and smug. Ha, I thought, those little witches wouldn't get the better of me. I opened a beer, pressed play, sat back and waited for my saviour to reveal herself. They didn't make a sound. Nothing. They couldn't have known they were being watched. How could they? Days passed... They never made another sound. I fed them, knowing that two of them were, as I saw it, scrounging, living off me with no way of ever paying me back. I got into debt to feed them. But I saw it as an investment, still hoping that one day I'd discover which was the one. I don't remember when it was that I started to notice that the street outside was getting busier. It happened slowly I suppose. But when it got difficult to get out of the house for all the people filling the pavement I knew that there was something going on. All the people were stood staring at my house and smiling. It was freaky, Eric. The radio reported that the roads all over the country were congested with people trying to get to the same destination: my house! People all over the world were trying to get here! It was then that I realised it was the triplets. It was their silence. It was their unity. That silence was more beautiful than the sweet noise that one of them could make, it was more beautiful than any noise, than any sound. That was the same day that I got the triplets the record deal. And the same day that I confessed to the cops. It was the silence I suppose. It had been working on me too. And so here I am. It's not so bad. Prisons are changing, like everything else on the planet. Everything is ascending. So that's my story, Eric. Are you going to play their record now?'

'Yes I am, Barry. It's strange to think that in a way the world has you to thank for the peace that The Triplets are bringing.'

'It's a strange world, Eric.'

'It sure is, Barry. But an increasingly happy one.'

'Goodbye Eric.'

'Goodbye Barry. So here it is. You are listening to Radio Noise and this is The Triplets' Silence...'

Escape from the Butcher's Shop

I was born in a butcher's shop and for many years believed myself to be nothing more than a lump of slowly decaying meat.

I was born between a string of pork sausages and a pile of lamb cutlets. My parents were butchers. They are dead now.

The butcher's shop never had any customers. The door was always locked and there were no windows.
'Perhaps this shop is all that exists,' I used to think.

I yearned for escape. It hurt to yearn. The more I yearned, the more pain I felt. Sometimes I wished that I could be satisfied with all that appeared to be, rather than yearning for more.
As the pain grew, I began to see that everything had a keyhole: every steak, every sausage, each of the four walls, the ceiling and the floor; everything had a keyhole from which shone bright, white light. It was impossible to look into that light without being blinded. I wanted to live within that light. Though the rest of the meat in the shop ignored it, I was entranced. I had to escape. I had to escape from the butcher's shop.
I jumped from my shelf to the sawdust-covered floor and ran to the door. It was bolted from the inside.

Apparently the only thing one needed to escape was the intention to escape. I slid the bolt, opened the door and walked outside.

I was free! I could hardly believe it. But then, as I looked around me, I saw that everything outside the butcher's shop had a keyhole too: every lamp post, every tree, even the pavement had a keyhole and so did the sky. I was not within the light. I had not escaped. The confines of the butcher's shop had simply grown.

I walked along the street.

A man approached me wearing a sandwich board printed with the words.

'Keyhole-plugs.'

'Keyhole-plugs!' he shouted. 'Keyhole-plugs! Get your keyhole-plugs! Every colour! They're lovely! Get your keyhole-plugs! Finest quality! Keyhole plugs!'

In each hand he carried a transparent polythene-bag containing many differently coloured, keyhole-shaped lumps of plastic. The keyhole in his forehead was filled with one of these objects, a blue one, preventing the light from shining out of it.

I walked away from the salesman and continued down the street towards a park. I entered the park and saw a man wearing a black suit, sitting on a bench and reading a newspaper. The keyhole in his forehead was filled with a red keyhole-plug. I decided to approach him.

'Excuse me, sir,' I said. 'Where am I?'

Without looking up, the man replied:

'In the butcher's shop, of course.'

'Yes,' I said, 'yes, of course. And if you don't mind me asking, who are you?'

'Who am I?' he said, 'Why, I am a lovely slice of veal. At a very reasonable price.'

'And who am I?' I asked.

He looked up from his newspaper, put a hand in front of his face as if shading his eyes from something, then looked me up and down.

'You are an off-cut,' he said with disdain, then tucked his newspaper under his arm, stood up and walked away.

I sat down on the bench, rested my head in my hands and cried.

After a while, I began to become aware of distant laughter. It grew louder and I raised my head to see where it was coming from. A young woman was walking through the park, pointing and laughing at everything around her. The light shone freely out of the keyhole in her forehead. People seemed to be avoiding her as if she was dangerous. She pointed at me and laughed.

'Who are you?' she asked.

'I'm an off-cut,' I said.

The woman laughed again.

'No you're not,' she said.

'What am I then?'

'Someone tried to create a thing without a keyhole once,' the woman said, suddenly serious. 'They tried to create something through which the light would not shine. It was impossible. How many keyholes does a lump of meat have?'

'One,' I said.

'Yes. If you take a cleaver and bring it down hard against that lump of meat, severing it in two, then how many keyholes does each piece of meat have?'

'One,' I said.

'Exactly. Everything has a keyhole.'

'So what am I?' I asked, confused.

The woman suddenly turned and started running away from me.

'Come on!' she called.

Not knowing what else to do, I followed. The woman led me through the park, then through many streets, then into a house.

'These are my parents,' she said, laughing as she pointed at an elderly couple sat in armchairs facing away from us.

The armchairs were facing a blank wall. The couple were staring at the blank wall with blank expressions.

They both had matching, grey keyhole-plugs in their foreheads. The man turned his head to look at us.

'Put your plug in!' he shouted at his daughter. 'You're a disgrace!'

The woman laughed. Her father scowled, then returned to looking at the wall.

The laughing woman took my hand, then led me into another room that was empty except for a mirror.

I saw myself in the mirror. There was a keyhole in my forehead. Of course there was. Everything has a keyhole. And yet I had never thought about myself having one, just everything else.

'Look through your keyhole,' the laughing woman said.

'But I'll be blinded.'

'That's what you think.'

I stepped closer to the mirror and closed one eye, then with the other, I looked through the light-emitting keyhole in my forehead. The light did not blind me. I could see my parents in the light. I turned from the mirror and looked through the keyhole in the laughing woman's forehead. There they were again. I looked through the keyhole in the mirror and I could see them; I looked through the keyhole in each of the walls and I could see them; I looked through the keyhole in the floor and I could see them and I looked through the keyhole in the ceiling and I could see them. I could see my parents through every keyhole and they didn't look like butchers anymore.

'Where is the key to all the keyholes?' I asked the laughing woman. 'Is my skeleton key-shaped? Is it a skeleton key? Will it be revealed when my flesh decays? Do I have to die to escape?'

'You do not need to escape at all,' the laughing woman said. 'Look!'

And suddenly all the keyholes grew to become the same size and shape as the objects that contained them so that there was nothing but light.

'Everything else is an illusion,' the laughing woman said and I realised that I was not trapped in a butcher's shop at all and that I never had been.

The End of the Pier

There was a life-sized picture of a fat woman and a skinny man, both wearing bathing costumes, painted on wood, with holes where their faces should have been. It was my job to charge people to stick their heads through the holes.

Phyllis made him kiss her... that's what I thought... I saw them on the dodgems... her and Steve.

I shouldn't have pushed Phyllis in the sea. I can say I'm sorry and mean it now, now that I can see through her face-hole as well as through mine. Now she can see through my face-hole too and she takes my sorry and kisses it. Kisses it! Hard to believe but true true true. Helps me *and* her. Couldn't do it when I was alive; too much stuff in the way.

One evening, Steve was sawing in his shed.
'What are you doing?' I said.
'Nothing that concerns you, nosy wife,' he said.
Then it was my birthday and he blindfolded me, walked me out into the garden, then took the blindfold off. There was a big present, bigger than me, all wrapped up pretty. I opened it and what was it? Only a life-sized picture of me, painted on wood, with a hole cut out where my face should have been! Ha ha ha! What a

laugh! Now everyone could have a go at being me... to see what it was like. And everyone did have a go! Betty, Rita, Big Cyril, Smelly Jim, even Mr Pickles... When Steve did it I felt the best. I wanted him to feel how I felt the most.

Now it's my turn, putting my head through the face-hole in everybody else, and seeing me looking back at them. Big truth makes me good, makes me lovely. My sorries are kissed and I'm kissing sorries.

They buried the picture of me after I took my head out of its face-hole. It never was me anyway... see that now. Been holding on to it all this time, holding on so hard it hurts. Don't need it no more.

Lesley Visits the Barbers

Lesley had never noticed the Unisex Barbershop before now. Yet as soon as the building had been noticed, it was as if it was all there was to see.

Lesley stared at the spiralling red and white stripes of the slowly rotating barber pole, entranced.

Getting a haircut was an odd decision for Lesley. There had not until now been anyone around to pass judgement upon Lesley's hair, no one to either admire it or ridicule it, so its appearance had never been important. Indeed, until now, Lesley had not even been aware that such a thing as appearance existed. No, there was really no reason for Lesley to get a haircut, but then what else was there to do?

'Hello!' the barber said, welcoming Lesley with open arms, the scissors in the barber's right hand snipping the air... snip, snip, snip...

Lesley stared at the snipping scissors. The barber followed Lesley's gaze and laughed.

'I was born with my right thumb and middle finger twitching,' the barber said, 'so my profession was inevitable. As soon as someone placed the handles of a pair of scissors over my twitching fingers everything else just fell into place.'

'I see,' said Lesley.

'They twitch constantly,' said the barber.

'I see,' said Lesley.

'Won't you sit down?' asked the barber.

'Thank you, yes,' Lesley said and sat in the barber's chair, facing a mirror on the wall.

The barber tied a white sheet around Lesley's neck.

'Short back and sides, please,' said Lesley.

'Certainly,' said the barber, 'but... before we begin... Are you a man?'

'I'm sorry?'

'Are you a man?'

'Yes,' said Lesley, taken aback. 'Of course I'm a man.'

'You're sure?'

'Yes, I'm sure.'

'You're not a man *and* a woman?'

'What?'

'You're not a man *and* a woman? You're not a hermaphrodite?'

'No! I am not a hermaphrodite! I am a man! Why are you asking me this? And what business is it of yours anyway?'

'Oh, it is fundamental to my business, madam.'

'Sir!'

'Just testing,' the barber said. 'So you are definitely a man. You're not a hermaphrodite.'

'I am definitely a man! I am not a hermaphrodite!'

'Splendid, splendid. That's wonderful... that's all I

wanted to know. But I've upset you. I'm sorry. Would you like a cup of tea? By way of an apology.'

The barber's left hand pointed at a pot of tea on a table.

'No, not really,' said Lesley. 'I just want a haircut.'

'It would really please me if you accepted my offer,' the barber said. 'I would feel so much better. Please.'

Lesley sighed.

'Very well. If it will make you feel better.'

'Excellent,' said the barber, then produced, from beneath the table, an enormous cup and saucer.

The barber poured the whole contents of the teapot into the cup.

'Milk and sugar?' the barber enquired.

'Yes, please,' said Lesley.

The barber added a little milk and a little sugar to the tea, then handed the brimming, oversized cup and saucer to Lesley.

Lesley was about to protest at the size of the vessel but, upon seeing the barber's pleading eyes, wearily accepted the offering, took it in both hands, then began to drink.

Slurp.

'It's very good,' Lesley said.

The barber smiled.

'I am glad that you like it,' the barber said. 'I will cut

your hair whilst you drink. Short back and sides wasn't it?'

'That's right, yes. Thank you.'

The barber moved the ceaselessly snipping scissors towards Lesley's hair.

Snip, snip, snip.

Slurp, slurp, slurp.

Snip, snip, snip.

'Finished,' the barber said.

Lesley looked at the mirror.

'Very good,' said Lesley, 'very good.'

'Something for the weekend, sir?'

'I'm sorry?'

'Something for the weekend?'

'What weekend?'

'Let me put it another way... Sheaths? Johnnies? Rubbers?'

'Oh, no thank you.'

'I don't just have condoms. I have various forms of contraceptives... for both men and women.'

Lesley turned around and glared at the barber.

'I wasn't suggesting...' the barber protested, 'I assure you... I'm through with all that. If you say that you are a man then you are a man. Case closed. I was just ensuring that you were aware that there are many ways to ensure that copulation does not result in...' the barber winced, '...procreation. I am the greatest exponent of contraception there is. I truly believe that no one should *ever* have sexual intercourse without using contraception.'

'Ever?'

'Ever!'

The barber's scissors continued to snip the air.

'Will there be anything else, sir?' the barber enquired.

In a hushed voice, Lesley said:

'Yes. Could I use your... er... facilities? All this tea...'

'Of course, sir, yes,' the barber said, smiling. 'No problem at all.'

The barber's left hand took the enormous, empty cup and saucer from Lesley and placed them back beneath the table. Then the barber's left hand untied the sheet from around Lesley's neck. Then the barber's left hand pointed at two doors either side of the mirror, one marked 'Gentlemen' and the other marked 'Ladies'.

Lesley stood up, looked at the doors, then turned around to face the barber and said:

'I don't know which one to use.'

'Aha!' the barber shouted. 'I knew it!'

Snip, snip, snip. The barber strode towards the hermaphrodite, the ceaselessly snipping scissors growing larger with every step, then...

Snip!

The barber cut the hermaphrodite in two, thus beginning the universe.

Extraordinary Elsie

The words 'Extraordinary Elsie' are written in yellow light-bulbs on the front of the theatre. Inside the theatre, the excited audience sits facing closed, red curtains. Now the curtains open to reveal a small, dishevelled, elderly woman wearing a thick overcoat and carrying a shopping bag. The audience gasps. Elsie looks back at the audience with complete bemusement.

Yesterday, when the audience read about Extraordinary Elsie on the poster pasted to the front door of the theatre, they could hardly believe it, but believe it they did.

A large, wooden crate is now wheeled onto the stage, pushed by none other than Basil Darlington, the owner of the theatre. The words 'Extraordinary Elsie' are painted on the front of the crate in yellow.

Elsie points at the words painted on the crate, then points at herself, whilst looking at Basil quizzically. Basil nods. Elsie looks back at him with complete disbelief. Do the words really refer to her?

Basil produces a large, gold key from his pocket, then unlocks and opens a door in the side of the crate. Elsie peers inside, then looks back at Basil with another quizzical look. Basil nods. Elsie steps inside the crate. Basil closes the door behind her, locks it, then stands facing the awe-struck audience, smiling and holding the gold key aloft.

A small boy now walks onto the stage with a drum hanging round his neck and a drumstick in each hand. With a nod from Basil, the boy begins a drum roll. The lights dim, leaving only a single spotlight illuminating the stage, where Basil continues to hold the gold key aloft, the boy continues his drum roll, and the wooden crate remains locked.

The audience holds its breath. The drum roll continues... and continues... and continues... The crate still remains locked. The audience exhales but continues to stare at the locked crate, transfixed, with complete faith in Elsie's extraordinariness.

Three minutes have now passed and the crate remains steadfastly shut. The drum roll begins to slow. Basil flashes a threatening look at the drumming boy who immediately resumes his speed in spite of the growing pain in his wrists and the tears welling in his eyes. The audience do not for a moment waver in their focused concentration upon the crate or in their continued expectation of Extraordinary Elsie living up to her name.

Three hours have now passed and Basil is ignoring the fact that the drum roll has slowed to an occasional, exhausted tap, for Basil is now also finding it difficult to fulfil his role. His arm that is holding the gold key aloft is slowly but surely descending and his smile is turning into a scowl. The audience, however, remain as positive and excited as they were when Elsie first appeared.

Three days have now passed. The audience are continuing their faithful vigil but Basil has had enough. He is staring at the locked crate with utter contempt. His once raised arm now hangs limp. He looks over at the drummer boy who is lying on the stage, fast asleep. Basil's fingers fall open and he drops the gold key to the floor. Now he turns his back on the audience, steps over the sleeping boy and walks off the stage.

Basil emerges from the theatre, blinking in the light. He hails a cab, rides silently home, steps inside his house, takes a gun from a cupboard and shoots himself dead.

Three years have now passed and the wooden crate in the theatre is still locked, with no sign of Extraordinary Elsie ever living up to her name. Yet the audience are still sat in their seats, all still staring at the crate and, though their health has deteriorated, their belief that Elsie is extraordinary has not deteriorated in the slightest.

Nine years have now passed and the audience contains children who were born in the theatre. The building's confines are all that the children know; as far as they are aware, life consists solely of sitting and staring at a locked, wooden box.

Nine years ago, Elsie entered the theatre through the back door. She had been on her way home from the supermarket when she had noticed the words written in yellow light-bulbs on the back of the theatre. The words read: 'The Extraordinary Audience'. When Elsie read about the audience on the poster pasted to the back door of the theatre, she could hardly believe it, but believe it she did.

Elsie is dead. The truth is, she died two minutes and fifty-nine seconds after the door of the crate was locked. Elsie's smiling spirit has been standing on top of the crate ever since her death, patiently waiting for The Extraordinary Audience to live up to its name.

In the audience, someone wheezes then slumps in their seat. This is the first member of the audience to die. Their faith in Elsie remained until the end and now their faith is proven to have been justified: as their spirit leaves their body, they see Elsie standing on top of the crate. The spirit of the dead audience member claps their hands, laughing and laughing. Elsie smiles.

One by one, the audience members die; one by one their spirits leave their bodies; and one by one they applaud Extraordinary Elsie.

 The smiling spirits of the audience leave the theatre through the back door, then turn and see their name up in lights; Elsie leaves the theatre through the front door, then turns and sees her name up in lights. Elsie and the audience can hardly believe who they are, but believe it they do.

Mask Man

Tom and Millie are constantly smiling. Tom and Millie are constantly happy.

Of the previous two statements, only one is true. Tom and Millie are indeed always smiling but Tom is certainly not always happy. Tom is in constant pain. Tom hides his pain behind his smiling face. His face is a mask: a mask that hides. Millie's face, however, does not hide. If Millie were ever unhappy, she would not hide her unhappiness, her smile would turn to a grimace. But she is always happy so she always smiles. Tom does not want her smile to turn to a grimace. That is why Tom hides his pain.

Tom's pain appeared last winter. Tom's doctor said that the pain is of bacterial origin.

'It's the fancy-dress party at the weekend, Tom. You should think about what you're going to go as,' Millie says.

'What are *you* going to go as?'

'A nurse.'

'Why a nurse?'

'I've always wanted to be one.'

Tom has bought some clay. He sits at the dining room table and kneads it. He wants to make a mask. He looks hard at the clay. The more he stares at it, the more he becomes aware of the pain that fills his body. Whilst he moulds the material, he does not think about the clay, he thinks about the pain, the way it feels, its particular... physiognomy. The clay begins to take the form of a face. Tom smoothes its surface, holds it at arm's length, then levels his gaze at its unseeing eyes.

'This is the face of the pain,' he thinks.

Tom pushes a skewer through each of the mask's pupils, then through each of its nostrils. Next, he makes two holes at the sides for elastic and one in the centre of the mouth. He then puts the mask in the oven and turns up the heat.

When it is dry, hard and cold, Tom paints the mask red, attaches a length of elastic to it, then tries it on in front of the mirror.

'This mask does not hide,' Tom thinks, 'it reveals.'

'Oh wow!' says Tom. 'You look fabulous.'

'Oh, so you have a nurse thing, huh?'

'Er... no, I mean I... maybe, I don't know, er...'

Millie kisses Tom's cheek.

'You look nice in your suit,' she says. 'Put your mask on.'

'OK.'

'You're scary,' Millie laughs, then kisses the mask on the

cheek.

Tom feels as if it is his pain that is being kissed and not him.

'Don't do that!' Tom shouts.

Millie backs away.

'Sorry,' Tom says. 'I didn't mean to shout. I didn't like that. Sorry.'

Millie frowns.

'OK,' she says.

It Is dark as Tom and Millie walk, hand in hand, through the town. It feels good to Tom to be wearing the mask and holding Nurse Millie's hand.

They arrive at the door of an enormous house. Millie knocks. The door opens.

'Hi Millie, nice outfit,' says a woman with wings and a halo.

'Hello,' Tom says, 'I'm Tom.'

The angel looks at Tom and her smile turns to a grimace. She says nothing.

'This is Tom,' Millie says, 'my husband.'

'Yes. Hello Tom. Sorry,' says the angel, 'it's just... I don't know whether Richard will see the funny side. Perhaps you know him better than I do. Come in, anyway, come in.'

Millie and Tom exchange a confused glance, then they

enter the house.

The angel leads Millie and Tom through a long hallway and into a huge room full of people in costumes, all chatting and drinking.

'Have fun,' the angel says, then leaves them.

'Who's Richard?' Tom asks Millie.

'I don't know. Let's not stay long. I've got a bad feeling about this.'

'Yes, I know what you mean.'

Tom picks up two glasses of red wine and hands one to Millie who has started chatting to another nurse. The two women compare each other's outfits.

An Egyptian mummy approaches Tom.

'You look like you could do with something stronger than that,' the mummy says, pointing at Tom's drink. 'I know *I* could. There is somewhere we could go.'

'I can't leave. I'm with my wife.'

'It's just another room. This is my party.'

'Oh. It's a great place you've got here.'

'Thanks. I moved in last winter.'

The mummy leads Tom through a red wallpapered corridor. At the end of the corridor is a wooden door. The mummy opens the door, then leads Tom into a small room covered in the same red wallpaper. An ornate, gold-framed mirror hangs on the far wall, above a wooden, fluted plinth. In the centre of the room is a wooden table and two wooden chairs. On the table is a white china plate and a silver knife and fork set for a meal.

'So what have you got?' Tom asks the mummy. 'I could certainly do with feeling better.'

The mummy does not answer. He sits down in the chair that faces the plate and cutlery.

Tom walks over to the plinth. On top of it is a petri-dish. Tom peers at its contents.

'What's this?' Tom asks. 'Some sort of fungus? Is this what we're going to take?'

'No,' says the mummy. 'That has already been taken. Sit down.'

Tom sits opposite the mummy, who stares at him in silence. Tom feels increasingly uncomfortable. Suddenly, the mummy takes hold of one of the bandages wrapped around his head, pulls it loose and begins to unwind it, eventually revealing a face that is inflamed, red and raw. The face looks exactly like Tom's mask.

'Oh!' Tom says, shocked.

Tom takes off his mask and places it face down on the table.

'I had no idea,' Tom says. 'This is a coincidence, a strange coincidence. I assure you I have never seen you before... I'm so sorry... I don't know what to say.'

The man stares intently at Tom's face, then says:

'My name is Richard.'

Richard unwinds the rest of his bandages, underneath which he is wearing an identical suit to Tom's.

The door opens and a woman enters. She is dressed as a dominatrix, in a tight, black, rubber dress. There is a black key hanging on a chain around her neck.

'Hi Ricky,' she says, draping her arms around Richard's neck and kissing his face.

'Is this woman in love with my pain?' Tom thinks.

'Not now,' Richard says and the woman reluctantly leaves, scowling at Tom as she does so.

Richard stands up.

'Wait for me here,' Richard says to Tom, then he leaves the room.

Tom breathes a sigh of relief, then picks up his mask, puts it back on, stands up, looks at himself in the mirror and thinks:

'What the hell is going on?'

Richard returns to the party. Millie ambles drunkenly towards him.

'Hello Tom,' she says. 'I thought I'd lost you.'

In the red wallpapered room, the wooden door opens

and the dominatrix re-enters. She looks at Tom quizzically.

'I thought you were going to wear your bandages,' she says.

Then she steps forward and kisses Tom's mask.

'Don't! Please don't do that,' Tom says.

'Why? What's wrong with you, Ricky? Why don't you want me to kiss you? What's this?' she asks and pulls at the mask's elastic.

The elastic breaks and the mask falls to the floor. The dominatrix screams, picks the mask up and hugs it to her chest whilst rocking back and forth.

At the party, Richard says to Millie:

'I have a secret to tell you.'

'Oh good,' Millie says, smiling, 'I like secrets. Well, the telling of them that is.'

'I am in constant pain,' Richard says.

Millie's smile turns to a grimace.

'Since when?'

'Last winter.'

'Why didn't you tell me?'

Richard does not answer.

'Oh Tom,' she says and wraps her arms around Richard's neck and kisses his cheek.

Richard suddenly feels hollow, and he feels that it is not

him that Millie is kissing but the empty space within him.

'Please don't do that,' Richard says. 'I don't like it.'

'Sorry darling,' Millie says. 'I forgot. Take your mask off so that I can kiss you properly.'

'I wish I could,' Richard says then turns and walks out of the room.

'Where are you going?' Millie calls.

Richard returns to the red wallpapered room. The dominatrix drops Tom's mask, throws her arms around Richard and kisses his face. Richard smiles.

'Kiss me again,' he says.

Although Richard feels that it is him that is being kissed and not the empty space inside him, the thought that the space inside him exists still remains and he wants it to be full. Richard picks Tom's mask up off the floor, sits down at the table and lays the mask on the china plate. Then, with the dominatrix standing at his side, he picks up the silver knife and fork, cuts off a slice of the mask, puts it in his mouth and swallows.

'That's clay,' Tom says.

Richard ignores him and cuts off another slice. With every mouthful that Richard swallows, Tom feels the pain within him decrease. Richard continues to eat the mask until the plate is empty, the space inside him is full and Tom feels no pain at all.

'Lock the door on your way out,' Richard says as he removes the black key from around the neck of the dominatrix and hands it to Tom.

'Thank you,' Tom says, then he leaves the room, locks the door behind him and puts the key in his pocket.

Behind the locked, wooden door, inside the red wallpapered room, Richard bursts into tears. Then, whilst the dominatrix sits in the corner and masturbates, Richard kneels down in front of the plinth and bows down to the bacteria in the petri-dish.

Tom walks back into the party, walks towards Millie and says:

'I think maybe I *have* got a bit of a nurse thing.'

The Unnameable Made Flesh

You see an advertisement but you don't know what it's for. It isn't like all the other ads. All the other ads advertise the same thing, though in different forms, they all advertise themselves. This ad is unique. It isn't many; it is one.

'Is there something missing from your life?' the ad says with a twinkling smile. 'Do you have the feeling that you have misplaced something but you don't know what it is? It's not your keys, you know where they are, they're in your pocket; it's not your porcelain flying duck, that's hanging on your wall. But something is missing. What is it?'

Then the ad looks straight at you, right into your eyes and says:

'This ad isn't for you! It's for everyone else! Go away!'

You walk on past the advertisement, towards the restaurant where you have arranged to meet your date. Listening to the ad has made you late. You see your date, a woman called Rhonda, standing outside the restaurant, waiting for you.

'Sorry I am late,' you say, holding out your right hand for her to shake.

'That's all right,' she says, smiling, but she ignores your hand.

You try to direct her attention to your waiting hand by

waggling the fingers but she continues to ignore it, though from her cheery smile it appears that she is not ignoring it out of anger.

'You're sure that you aren't upset that I am late?' you say, your proffered hand still outstretched.

'No,' she says, still smiling. 'Not at all.'

'Good,' you say.

You notice that Rhonda's right hand, unlike her clean, manicured left hand, is dirty and the nails are so long that they spiral in on themselves as if they have never been cut.

'Shall we go in?' she asks.

You reluctantly lower your unshaken right hand.

Inside the restaurant, you and Rhonda sit opposite one another and order. When the food comes, Rhonda picks up her knife in her left hand, cuts up her food, then puts her knife down and picks up her fork, again with her left hand. Her dirty, long-nailed right hand hangs limp, unused. You wonder whether it is crippled in some way, perhaps paralysed.

You pick up your fork in your left hand, then your knife in your right hand. Rhonda stares at your knife and screams. In shock, you drop your cutlery.

'That knife just levitated!' Rhonda says.

'This knife?' you say, picking it up in your right hand

again and holding it aloft.

Rhonda screams again and runs out of the restaurant.

As you walk home, you notice that everyone you pass has an unwashed, long-nailed right hand that hangs limp, unused.

You pass a glove shop. All the gloves in the window are for left hands.

You pass the advertisement that made you late. It addresses the people around you:

'What is it that is missing?' it asks. 'What is it?'

At home you turn on the television. It's that new, animated soap opera, the one that everyone says is *so* realistic. It's called 'The Way Things Are'. All of the characters have no right hands.

The doorbell rings. It is Rhonda.

'Sorry I took off like that,' she says. 'I was spooked by that levitating knife. You must think I'm crazy but I know what I saw. Oh!' she exclaims, seeing the television. 'It's The Way Things Are! It's *so* realistic!'

She sits down and stares at the television. You place your right hand in front of her eyes. It does not interrupt her viewing at all. She appears to be able to see right through it. You remove your hand from in front of her eyes then stand between her and the television.

'I have a right hand,' you say.

'What?' she exclaims, then laughs.

'It's like this one,' you say, holding up your left hand, 'but it's reversed and is situated on the end of my right arm.'

She stares at you.

'You think your stump has fingers?' she says. 'Oh wow! You're totally whacko!'

Then her laughing face changes to compassion.

'Oh,' she says. 'You're serious. You must be sick.'

Then her compassionate face changes to horror as her consciousness expands and she becomes aware of your right hand, hearing its name having made it visible.

She looks at your right hand as if it is a superfluous appendage, as if it is a third hand. Then she looks down at her own dirty, long-nailed, unused right hand and screams. She has never seen it before. She turns away from it and shuts her eyes.

'It isn't real, it isn't real!' she says in desperation.

You kneel down before her and take hold of her right hand in your own.

'I can feel it!' she says, terrified.

You kiss her right hand's palm.

'Get away from me!' she shouts.

She opens her eyes then runs into the kitchen. You

hear the knife drawer open. You hear a scream. You run into the kitchen. She has amputated her right hand. Now she looks like one of the characters from 'The Way Things Are', except for all the blood.

'That won't get rid of it,' you say. 'You can still feel it, can't you?'

'Yes,' she whispers. 'It's... beautiful... but it's wrong.'

'It's nothing to be afraid of,' you say. 'It's you.'

Clutching her bleeding stump, she shouts:

'You've made me a freak! I never want to see you again!' then she leaves.

After leaving your house, Rhonda walks straight to the nearest police station.

The following day, the unique advertisement is demolished; a new law is passed making the use of the words 'right hand' illegal; and a small emergency guillotine stands on every street-corner, ready to amputate all that threatens the state's power.

Now you are lying in your bed. Your body is decaying. Your feet fade away first, then your legs disappear, then your genitals, then your left hand and arm, then your torso, then your neck, then your head, then your right arm, until all that is left is your right hand. Your right hand does not decay, cannot decay, it cannot die. It is you. Its fingers curl into its palm then it gives a thumbs-up.

Stan and Stan

Stan works in a factory, on the assembly line, ensuring that all the products are identical. He takes great pleasure in destroying any anomalies.

Stan wears his clothes inside out. He has done so ever since he first met his wife, Marjory. Marjory's first words to Stan were:
'Your clothes are inside out.'
Previously unaware of the mistake, Stan covered up the weakness it revealed by pretending that it was intentional.
'I always wear my clothes inside out,' he lied. 'I prefer it.'
Stan ensured that from that day on he always wore his clothes inside out.

On their first date, Marjory asked Stan:
'Do you like my hair?'
To which Stan replied:
'I'd prefer it if it was more like mine.'

Walking home from the factory, Stan says to himself:
'I wonder if we'll get through this evening without an argument.'
When he reaches home, Marjory is sat at the dining table, knitting a tiny pair of pink and blue striped socks.

Not noticing Marjory's activity, Stan says:

'There was a fight at work today. It was horrible. I started to have an attack but I managed to look at my mirror before it got too bad.'

'Good,' Marjory says.

'How I long for unity,' Stan says.

'We could create unity right now, Stanley,' Marjory says. 'We could make a baby!'

Stan stares at her, appalled.

'Why must you insist on driving us apart?' he yells. 'Why must you be so different from me? You are supposed to be my wife! When I say I want unity, I mean similarity. I do not want some hybrid offspring. How can there ever be peace in this world if everyone insists on being so different from one another!'

Stan is beginning to hyperventilate. He leaves the room and slams the door. Marjory angrily resumes her knitting with renewed vigour.

Stan fumbles in his inside-out trousers' pocket and produces a small mirror. He looks at his reflection and calms. His breathing slowly returns to normal.

'No-one sees things the way I do,' Stan says to himself. 'Talk to anyone for long enough and you'll end up disagreeing. We are all alone.'

Stan leaves the house by the back door and walks through the garden to his shed.

Inside his shed, Stan plucks a hair from his head, then carefully places it in a test-tube full of green liquid. He seals the test-tube with a cork, then places it on the floor inside a large, metal cage.

Later that evening, when Stan and Marjory are sat in their living room, Stan announces:

'My brother is visiting tomorrow.'

'Your brother?' Marjory says, putting down the tiny, pink and blue striped hat that she has been knitting, 'You don't have a brother.'

'Marjory, what are you saying? I have a twin brother, you know that.'

'A twin? What are you talking about? You've never mentioned that before!'

'Oh Marjory, don't be ridiculous. Do you really think I would neglect to tell you something as important as that? You worry me sometimes. I think you may be losing your mind. Anyway,' Stan says, 'I thought he could stay in the spare room.'

'But that was to be the nursery,' Marjory says. 'Have you *really* got a twin brother? Am I *really* losing my mind?'

'I have an identical twin brother,' Stan says, 'and he's coming to stay. It's going to be great!'

The next day, after work, when Stan reaches his house, he walks straight through the front door and out of the back door, without acknowledging Marjory, then he walks inside his shed. Inside the cage is sat a naked man. The hair that was inside the test-tube is now growing from the naked man's head; the test-tube is in pieces on the floor.

'Oh my!' Stan says. 'How you've grown! You're... beautiful! I shall call you...Stan.'

The man inside the cage looks identical to Stan. He raises his head, looks through the bars at Stan and says:

'Why are you inside a cage?'

'I'm not,' Stan says, 'you are.'

'I beg to differ,' the clone says.

Stan unlocks and opens the cage, then hands the clone a shirt and a pair of trousers identical to his own. The clone puts the clothes on. Stan looks at the clone's clothes, then looks at his own inside-out clothes and says:

'You are more me than me. You are one less lie.'

Stan reaches out and takes his clone by the hand. The clone's hand feels eerily familiar to Stan. It feels to Stan as though he should have feeling in the clone's hand as well as in his own.

Stan leads the clone out of the shed, through the garden and into the house. He shows the clone what is behind every door in the house, finally ending with the living room.

'Marjory, this is my brother: Stan,' Stan says.

Marjory gasps and drops her knitting.

'What's wrong with your face?' the clone asks Marjory.

'Wrong with my face?' Marjory says, walking to one of the many mirrors in the house. 'Nothing's wrong with my face.'

'It's all wrong,' the clone says. 'It's the wrong shape and the eyes are the wrong colour and your hair is the wrong colour too. In fact your whole body is wrong. What are those two lumps on your chest?'

'Stanley!' Stan admonishes his clone. 'That is no way to speak to my wife. Go to your room!'

The clone turns and trudges sullenly upstairs to the nursery. Stan follows. When they reach the top of the stairs, the clone walks into the nursery, then turns around to face Stan and says:

'I like your house very much but I don't like that room,' and he points down the stairs at the front door, 'It's too big and it's full of anomalies.'

'Anomalies?' Stan queries.

'Yes,' the clone says. 'You know, like your wife.'

Stan and his clone stare at one another, in silence, across the threshold of the doorway, then Stan shuts the bedroom door.

'Goodnight Stan.'
'Goodnight Stan.'

The next morning, Marjory is sat at the breakfast table in the kitchen when Stan the clone enters and sits down opposite her. Deeply unsettled at being alone with the strange replica, Marjory stands up and calls:

'Stanley!'

'Yes?' the clone answers.

Marjory looks at the clone's clothes.

'You are not Stanley!' she says. 'And take off that hat and those socks, they are not for you!'

The clone removes the pink and blue striped, knitted hat and socks that he has stretched over his head and feet and Marjory snatches them from him.

'Stanley!' Marjory calls again.

Stan enters the room.

'Yes?'

Marjory desperately tries to put her feelings into words.

'I don't know,' she says.

Stan sighs and leaves for work.

The next morning, Stan wakes to find that he is alone in bed. Confused, he walks downstairs, calling:

'Marjory!'

Stan enters the living room where he sees his clone

calmly sat in his wife's armchair.

'Where is my wife?' Stan demands.

'I put her in the big room with all the others,' the clone says and points at the front door, from which Stan can now hear a loud knocking.

'Let me in!' he hears Marjory call through the door.

Stan tries to open the door but is unable. Stan's clone smiles, then says proudly:

'I nailed the door to the frame.'

Stan grabs his clone's hand and pulls him up from the armchair, drags him out of the back door, through the garden, then pushes him inside the shed and locks the door.

'I don't understand you!' Stan and his clone both shout in unison at one another through the locked door between them.

When Stan arrives home from work, he finds the shed door broken and a hole in the garden fence. He looks inside the shed. It is empty. He steps through the hole in the fence and out onto the street.

'Stan!' Stan calls. 'Stan! Where are you?'

Stan walks down the street, calling his own name, then he sees his clone shouting at strangers:

'Anomalies!' Stan's clone shouts. 'You are all anomalies!'

Stan removes a pistol from his inside-out trousers'

pocket and points it at his clone.

'I am not like you,' Stan says to his clone. 'I am not like you at all!'

'I am more you than you,' Stan's clone says, pointing at his clothes. 'Remember?'

'You are not me!' Stan shouts, then he shoots his clone in the chest.

Stan's clone smiles, apparently unharmed. Stan begins to hyperventilate. He produces his mirror from his Inside-out trousers' pocket and looks at his reflection. He has a bullet-hole in his chest. Stan looks away from the mirror, confused. He sees a passing cat.

'You are not me!' Stan shouts at the cat, then shoots it.

The cat runs away, unharmed.

Stan looks at his mirror again and sees that he now has two bullet-holes in his chest. He looks away from the mirror and sees a tree.

'You are not me!' Stan shouts at the tree, then aims his pistol at its trunk and shoots it.

Stan looks at his mirror again and sees that a third bullet-hole has appeared in his chest. He falls to his knees and looks up at the sky.

'You are not me!' Stan shouts at the sky, then shoots at it.

Stan looks at his mirror and sees that a fourth bullet-hole has appeared in his chest.

Then Stan suddenly realises who he really is. He laughs, drops his pistol, looks at the mirror in his corpse's hand and sees that he now has no reflection.

Insensible Susan

I looked after Susan for seventeen years. It was hard work because I had to do it on my own. Susan's dad passed away the day before she was born. I am Susan's mum. My name is Gloria.

Susan was born without any senses. She could not see; she could not hear; she could not taste; she could not smell; she could not feel.

Sometimes, at the end of a particularly tiring day, I wished that I too had no senses. It was a terrible thing to wish for and I never really meant it but, during those difficult moments, I thought that I did.

Susan was not paralysed. Her limbs flailed, her neck turned from side to side, her eyes rolled around. She moved about almost constantly but her movements were random.

Susan was not dumb either. She made random noises almost constantly too.

Three months ago, Susan made a noise that sounded like a word.

'Mission!' she shouted.

I dropped the bowl of porridge I was feeding her. It was impossible that she had said a word, of course. There was no way for her to know what a word was, let alone know that she was saying one. And yet, if there was just the smallest chance that she had gained even the tiniest amount of sensory awareness then I wanted to know about it. So I called her doctor. After a great deal of persuading, he reluctantly did some tests, which proved unequivocally that there was absolutely no change in her condition and that there was absolutely no way that she was able to perceive anything at all. Susan had no senses, she had never had any senses and she never would have any senses. Her saying the word had therefore either been a random coincidence or I had imagined it.

However, one week later, when I was washing her, it happened again. And it wasn't just a word this time but a sentence. In amongst the usual meaningless noises, she shouted:

'I am on a mission!'

I dropped the flannel.

'What sort of mission?' I asked, to which she replied:

'Splurrr...' then sicked up her breakfast.

For the rest of the day, I listened to her intently, hoping to hear something else intelligible but of course there was nothing.

Then, the following evening, when I was putting her to bed, she shouted:

'I am on a mission to free the prisoner!'

Over the next few days, I became quite used to occasionally hearing coherent sentences amongst her gibberish.

'I will complete my mission!' she said and 'The prisoner will be freed!'

The way that she spoke was so melodramatic that it sometimes made me laugh. I shouldn't have laughed, I know, but it was as if she thought she was some sort of hero and she was so far from being a hero that it was ridiculous.

'The time has come!' she said. 'Stand back faithful admirers, stand back sceptical cynics, stand back indifferent bystanders, I am about to take off!'

Then her arms flailed and the porridge spilt all over the bed.

One day, she kept repeating the same sentence:

'I am flying high in the sky, searching for the prison.'

Then, a few days later, in the middle of the night, I heard her shout:

'I have found the prison!'

I suppose you could say that, just as some of the random gibberish Susan spoke was bound to occasionally sound like words, so too some of the random movements she made were bound to occasionally look like actions but what happened next was so unbelievable that there must have been more than chance at work.

She was lying on her bed, porridge all around her mouth, seemingly oblivious to the random noises her voice was making and the random movements her body was making, when suddenly her legs swung over the side of the bed and she stood up. She stood up! A random movement? Perhaps. But then, as I watched, dumbstruck, she calmly walked out of the room.

She had no way of knowing that the room existed, let alone where the door was. Yet she calmly walked out of the room.

I followed.

'I am digging a hole in the ground!' she shouted as she walked into the living room.

'I am digging deeper!' she shouted as she picked up three boxes of incontinence pads, two boxes of porridge oats and a box of tissues, then piled them on top of one another in the middle of the coffee table.

'I am digging deeper!' she shouted as she walked into the kitchen.

'I am digging deeper!' she shouted as she opened a cupboard and removed three packets of flour and a packet of salt.

'I am digging deeper!' she shouted as she emptied the packets into a mixing bowl, then half-filled it with water.

'I am digging deeper!' she shouted as she stirred the

concoction with a wooden spoon.

'The hole is now a tunnel!' she shouted, then she carried the bowl into the living room and tipped the thick paste all over the pile of boxes on the coffee table.

'I am tunnelling under the prison!' she shouted as she walked back into the kitchen.

'I am tunnelling up through the floor of the prison!' she shouted as she opened a drawer and picked out a teaspoon.

'I have emerged from the tunnel inside the prison!' she shouted as she walked back into the living room.

'I am leading the prisoner down into the tunnel!' she shouted as she sculpted the homemade clay with the teaspoon.

'I am emerging from the tunnel with the prisoner!' she shouted as she dropped the teaspoon onto the floor.

I never used to believe that there was anything beyond what my senses can perceive. After Jim died, I could not see him, hear him, smell him, taste him or feel him, so how could he be?

Susan sculpted the clay until it looked like a man, until it looked like Jim, my husband, Susan's dad. I looked at the statue's face and tears came to my eyes.

'My mission is complete,' Susan said, then she collapsed

onto the floor and died.

I used to think that it was my shock at Jim's death that had caused Susan to be born the way that she was. I don't believe that any more.

She *was* on a mission, my Susan. And she completed it. And I am so very grateful to her. She *is* a hero.

Now, with no Susan to look after, I just get on with my life as best I can. I go to the shops; I watch television; on Wednesdays I play Bingo. But whenever I look at the statue in my living room, I wonder: what is it that I am *really* doing?

Harry's Quest

In the nursery, one year-old Harry picks up two wooden blocks, holds one in each hand, then bangs them together, over and over again, becoming more and more frustrated. Harry bangs the blocks together with an expression that suggests that he is trying to achieve something. When anyone tries to take the blocks away from him, he screams.

In the primary school playground, Harry walks up to a girl that he likes and asks her if she will play a game with him. The girl's name is Sarah. Sarah likes Harry and so agrees. Harry positions Sarah in the middle of the playground, walks as far away from her as possible, then turns around and faces her. Harry then runs as fast as he can towards her.

The last time that Harry ever saw Sarah was when she was looking at him through the back window of the ambulance.

Harry achieves a place at university to study physics. However, he attends very few of the lectures. Instead, he spends his time working on a lengthy dissertation that explores how separate, solid objects might be made to occupy the same space.

He does not pass the course.

Harry lies in his bed in the nursing home, barely breathing, feeling completely alone and a total failure. In utter despair, he gives up. In this moment of surrender, he suddenly becomes aware of an aura emanating from his body. The aura emanates from his body in all directions and penetrates all matter. It passes through the walls, floor and ceiling of the nursing home, through the sky and through the Earth and out into space. The aura passes through the moon, through the sun, and through the stars. It fills the whole universe, becoming increasingly subtle the further away that it extends from its densest part, its centre, Harry's body. Harry realises that this aura is as much a part of him as his body. Harry realises that he fills the universe.

The door to Harry's room opens and a nurse enters carrying a cup of orange squash and a pink wafer-biscuit. Harry sees a similar aura emanating from the nurse. In this moment, Harry suddenly knows that everyone in the universe has an aura emanating from them, each one filling the whole universe. Harry smiles, then beckons the nurse to come closer. She places the cup of squash and the wafer-biscuit on Harry's bedside-table, then she kneels down next to the bed and brings her ear close to Harry's mouth.

'We all already occupy the same space,' Harry whispers. 'It is just our centres that are at different points.'

120

The Living Crown

No one looks up, here. We daren't. We bow our heads out of deference, out of fear.

It is said that someone once looked up and saw it and survived. But that is probably just a story.

Outside, everyone hurries between the buildings as quickly as possible, all with bowed heads. Inside, we cower under the thick roofs.

We all do only what is expected of us. No one ever expresses dissent. No one ever dares to think that things can be different. We never look up.

Everyone knows who is in charge, of course. Everyone knows who is maintaining it all, who is enforcing it, who is controlling it. It is the one that we dare not look upon, the one who is above us all: the Living Crown.
What is the Living Crown? It is a huge crown of living flesh and bone that hovers above the city.

The Living Crown is deaf, dumb and blind but even if it could see, hear and speak I doubt that it would respond to our pleas, to our screams for mercy. For it does not care. It is a sadistic despot. It remains rigid and immobile, inflexible. It is a despicable monstrosity, an abomination. And down here everyone suffers.

I hate my life. I hate my flat, my job, my colleagues, the city... and most of all I hate the one that has made it so. I hate the Living Crown.

These thoughts are dangerous. In thinking these thoughts I have transgressed something. I have transgressed the Living Crown's law. Where will these illicit thoughts lead me? To madness or death no doubt.

I want to kill it. I want to shoot it from the sky. I want to see it fall. I want to watch it smash against the ground. Then I want to watch it rot. I want children who are not yet born to point in wonder at its skeleton, amazed at the size of it and shocked at how people could have ever lived beneath it. I want a national holiday to be declared on the day of its demise, to be celebrated annually with street parties in which every free and happy child, woman and man will look up. They will all look up. Everyone will look up. Oh how I want to kill it.

Old Farrahgate says that she lives down Shadowside; Ted Withers says that she has a flat in the Underhall; the Tefnall sisters say that she is dead; Sindy says that she never existed at all. But there is a small cottage down through the Twitten that is said to have a window in its roof. It is there that my thoughts are leading me.

I leave my flat and, with my head of course bowed, I turn towards the outskirts. The pavements are not as clean as in the centre of the city and they are covered in fewer advertisements.

I leave the pavements behind completely and follow a path lined with brambles and nettles. I arrive at a small cottage overgrown with ivy. I knock on the door.

After some considerable time, the door is opened by someone wearing green slippers. I raise my eyes a little and see that the slippers belong to a woman wearing a green frock. I raise my eyes a little more and see that the woman is elderly and that she is looking straight at me and smiling. Then she looks just above my head and scowls.

'You people with your ridiculous hats,' she says. 'What do you want?'

I frown.

'But I'm not wearing a hat,' I say.

'No of course you're not,' she says. 'What do you want?'

'Is it true that you once looked up?' I ask.

The woman smiles.

'It is,' she says.

I gasp then blurt out:

'I want to know about the Living Crown. I want to know exactly how high above the ground it is and I want to know its exact dimensions... I want to know everything about it so that... so that...' my voice lowers to a whisper... 'so that I can kill it.'

I suddenly cover my mouth with my hand. I am shocked at hearing myself say the words. But I also feel excitement. I have transgressed the Living Crown's law further and it is thrilling. For good or for bad, my life is changing now. The rigid state that it has been in for so long is being shaken.

The woman raises an eyebrow and gives a little smirk.

'And how are you going to do that?'

'I am going to build a weapon and I am going to shoot it. I am going to shoot the Living Crown out of the sky. But I need to know its exact specifications. Can you help me? Please?'

'Why don't you come in?'

I follow the woman through the doorway and into the little cottage.

'Nice carpet,' I say politely.

'Carpets, pavements, roads...' she spits, 'that's all you people care about.'

She leads me into a cosy living room with two armchairs and beckons me to sit opposite her.

'So,' she says, staring at me, 'you are here because I

125

dared to look up.'

'Yes.'

'And because you want to destroy the Living Crown.'

'Yes.'

'Because you blame it for your suffering.'

'Yes.'

'The ceiling of this room is made of glass.'

'What?'

I panic and stare fixedly at the carpet. Why hadn't she warned me? What if I had looked up at the ceiling? What if I had tripped and fallen onto my back? I feel nauseous and take deep breaths.

When I have calmed, I look back at the old woman. She is looking up. *She is looking up!*

I am terrified. The woman even appears to be smiling!

'Doesn't it scare you to look at it?' I ask. 'It is said that the sight of it can kill a person! Or make one mad!'

'Well,' she says, still looking up and smiling, 'maybe I am mad. Or maybe I am dead. But there is nothing to fear. Look up.'

Look up? I had not thought that my thoughts would lead me to this! I had not thought that I would have to look upon the monstrosity myself! Why do I have to look at it? Why can't she just give me the necessary information? And anyway, I think, why should I trust her? Perhaps she has never even seen the Living Crown.

Perhaps the ceiling isn't made of glass. Or perhaps she is blind, a blind killer who murders her victims by tricking them into looking up at the hideous thing.

'I can't,' I say, 'I just can't.'

Then suddenly she says:

'There is no Living Crown.'

'What?' I say, then I laugh at the preposterous statement. 'Then who is in charge?'

'If you are not at peace then it is you who is in charge. Are you at peace?'

'No I am not at peace,' I say, 'but I am certainly not in charge! I am not making myself suffer! Why would I?'

'If you are not in charge then why are you wearing that crown?'

'What?'

She *is* mad, I think to myself.

'That crown on your head,' she says. 'Why are you wearing it? You've been wearing it all your life. You were taught to make it, then to wear it, then to be unaware of it.'

Though I protest and protest, I somehow know that she speaks the truth. I break down and cry.

'If I am in charge,' I say, 'then overthrow me. Punish me, hurt me, destroy my will and replace it with yours. Tell me what to do. I will gladly be your slave.'

'That is not the way,' she says gently.

'Please!' I say. 'Remove the crown from my head! I no longer want to be the torturer and the tortured! Take it off! Take it off!'

'I cannot,' she says. 'You have to remove your crown yourself.'

'But how?' I protest. 'I have no awareness of it. I don't know where I end and it begins.'

'Look up!' she shouts at me. *'Look up!'*

My body shakes as I slowly bend back my neck and raise my eyes towards the ceiling. The ceiling is indeed made of glass. I look through it. *I look up!* And there it is... no crown of living flesh and bone hovering in the sky... nothing. There is no Living Crown.

I look up at the space where the Living Crown should be and I see something else there: I see the empty space that fills everything and that everything fills and I think:

'That is the true ruler!'

Instead of being rigid, it is formless; instead of controlling, it is freeing. It is not a part of everything that controls everything; it is the whole of everything that controls nothing. And it lives!

I look at that space and I speak to it, I say:

'Let your will be my will.'

And suddenly I feel a weight upon my head. I raise my hands towards that weight and my fingers touch something cold and hard. I lift the object down from upon me, then I lower my head to look at it and I see a gold crown. I throw it on the floor.

The old woman embraces me, then I leave the cottage, smiling.

As I walk freely through the streets, between the many kings and queens all wearing their gold crowns, some rich, some poor but all ruling themselves, I gaze up at the beautiful, empty sky. To all the kings and queens, the old woman and I *are* mad, to them we *are* dead. But I am not mad and I am not dead. My will is now our will, everything's will, the will of the true living crown. I have abdicated.

The End of Sex

It was raining as always but Brian didn't care because he had a new neighbour. Brian liked his new neighbour as soon as he saw her; he liked her a lot. He watched her move her belongings in to her new house, then he plucked up the courage to knock on her door.

'Hello,' he said, 'I'm Brian. I live next door.'

'Hello,' his new neighbour said, 'I'm Bryony.'

'Brian and Bryony,' said Brian, 'that's funny.'

'It is funny, yes.'

'I don't have a penis,' said Brian.

'Oh,' said Bryony.

'But it doesn't matter because if I really need one I just borrow one from my friend Doug round the corner. He's got three.'

'I see.'

There was a pause whilst Brian looked thoughtful, then he said:

'Did I say penis?'

'Yes, you did.'

'I meant to say umbrella.'

Embarrassed, Brian turned around and hurried back home.

'I need never see her again,' Brian said to himself.

There was a knock on Brian's door. He opened it. It was Bryony.

'I'm so sorry,' Brian said.

'Don't be,' said Bryony, 'Everything happens for a reason. Perhaps secretly you wish that you didn't have a penis.'

'You're right!' Brian said. 'I *do* secretly wish that I didn't have a penis! I don't like the feeling of desire. I wish that I wanted nothing.'

Then suddenly embarrassed at his outburst, Brian said: 'Sorry,' and shut the door.

There was another knock at the door. Brian opened it. It was Bryony again.

'I know exactly what you mean,' Bryony said. 'I wish that I didn't have a vagina.'

'Oh,' said Brian. 'Would you like to come in?'

Three hours later, Brian and Bryony were naked and approaching orgasm. They climaxed simultaneously, then parted and lay next to one another.

'That was incredible,' said Brian.

'It certainly was,' said Bryony.

'I can still feel myself inside you,' said Brian.

'I can still feel you inside me,' said Bryony.

Brian and Bryony looked down at their groins. Brian's penis was missing and Bryony's vagina was plugged up.

At the moment of orgasm, Brian's penis had broken off inside Bryony's vagina.

The couple looked out of the window. At last it had stopped raining.

Brian's penis remained embedded in Bryony's vagina for the rest of their lives, which they both went on to live in total satisfaction.

The Shining Flower

The Shining Flower has the same number of petals as it has roots; its stem is bent into a circle; each of its roots is growing from each of its petals. The Shining Flower is growing from itself and towards itself. And, of course, the Shining Flower is shining.

Although you did not see me, yesterday I ran towards you. When I reached you, I stood still, breathing quickly and heavily.

'I am not out of breath,' I said between gasps. 'I appear to be out of breath because you assume that I should be but in fact I have no breath to be out of. You see, although you imagine my form, I exist independently from it. Although I appear to be a postman, I am not a postman. I have taken a form that is appropriate for this meeting but I can take any form. My form is meaningful; it is symbolic of my nature. Like a postman, I am a messenger. I am a messenger from the Shining Flower. This is for you,' I said and showed you a letter.

Though you did not see it, the letter read:

'To whom it may concern,

Tomorrow you will read a story about me.

Yours sincerely,

The Shining Flower.'

Then I smiled, turned around and ran back towards the Shining Flower, from which I had come, becoming a part of it once more.

Look inside yourself now and see a flower. Not a shining flower, just an ordinary flower of a recognisable species. See it now in your mind. What species is it? What colour is it?

Why do you see the flower that you see and not another?

Now there is a whole garden of different flowers inside the readers of this story, all separated from one another by time and space.

Anyway, here's a story:

In a small village somewhere in England, the men are preparing for the annual Best Beard Championship. They have all spent the past months carefully tending their facial hair, training and trimming it, all hoping to be the one to defeat the ten years undefeated reigning champion: Lord Laurence Digby.

Lord Digby was born with a beard. Even stranger is that the young lord's beard was of such a length when he emerged from the womb that it would have taken not just nine months to grow but nine years. There are doctors who still shudder and reach for the brandy at the mere mention of it. Lord Digby himself does not believe the story, for he is a rational fellow. To maintain his rationality, he destroys all evidence to the contrary, burning any photographs of himself as a baby that he finds.

A stage has been erected in front of the village hall and a large, excited crowd has gathered to watch as, one by one, the hopeful participants step up onto the stage to show off their facial growths.

This year, there is a surprise entrant in the form of Barnaby the local beekeeper. Barnaby is something of a joke in the village on account of the fact that he does not appear to actually own any bees. He owns five hives but all appear to be completely empty. And yet he makes a living from selling honey. Where does it come from? The rest of the village have their suspicions. No sooner has Barnaby entered the local supermarket than the store detective leaps into action, guarding the sandwich-spread section with fierce vigilance.

What is particularly strange about Barnaby's entrance into the Best Beard Competition is that he is completely bald. He has not even one single whisker growing from his face. As he steps up onto the stage, the crowd begins to giggle then boo. But Barnaby is not perturbed. Ignoring the audience's abuse, he proudly sticks out his chin and strikes various poses.

Every year, Lord Digby sculpts his extraordinary facial bush as one might prune a privet hedge. His skill has increased over the years, having begun with mere geometric shapes, then progressed on to animals. This year, however, he believes that he has surpassed himself. He is certain that he will retain his title, having sculpted his beard into an extraordinarily realistic tableau depicting the coronation of her majesty Queen Elizabeth the Second. Elizabeth is sitting on her throne in the centre. To her right is the Archbishop of Canterbury holding the crown just above her head and flanked by two attendant choirboys.

The crowd applauds. No-one can deny the artistry, ingenuity, nay audacity of the extraordinary piece, but it is not until Lord Digby plays his trump card that the crowd is truly awestruck. By pulling on a fishing-wire that he has carefully secreted in his trouser pocket, Lord Digby elicits the effect of the archbishop slowly lowering the crown onto her majesty's head. The audience erupts into ecstatic cheers and everyone, including the other competitors, all agree that there is no question of the title of Best Beard being taken away from this master of facial-hair topiary.

Lord Digby nods in approval at the crowd's decision.

'I would like to congratulate you all,' he says, 'on choosing the only possible winner. But I have to say that my confidence was considerably shaken by one particular entrant this year. I am talking, of course, about Barnaby the beekeeper.'

The crowd bursts into laughter at the Lord's cruel sarcasm.

'Perhaps you could come on up here again Barnaby, to let us all feast our eyes once more upon your wondrous whiskers!'

The crowd guffaws as Barnaby obligingly steps up onto the stage, apparently oblivious to the ridicule.

'So, Barnaby,' Lord Digby says, 'perhaps you could tell us a little about this extraordinary beard of yours. What do you call this original style?'

'Bees,' says Barnaby.

'Bees?' enquires Lord Digby.

'Bees,' says Barnaby, 'transparent bees. I have a beard of transparent bees.'

Lord Digby and the crowd laugh even harder, tears running down their faces, slapping their thighs, then falling over and rolling on the ground in hysteria. But then... the laughing subsides, as everyone becomes aware of another sound, a buzzing sound. It grows slowly louder as the swarm of transparent bees leaves Barnaby's face, flies over the crowd, then out of this story altogether and towards its readers. The transparent bees fly towards you; they fly into your mind and towards the flower that is growing inside you.

The transparent bees fly from reader to reader, from flower to flower, cross-pollinating. As a result of this cross-pollination, you feel a significant growth in empathy towards your fellow readers, feeling closer and closer to them... almost one.

Now you see the flower inside you wither and die, to be replaced (as a result of the cross-pollination) by a new, hybrid flower, the like of which you have never seen before: a transparent flower. So now, dear readers, you all have the *same* flower inside you.

Now the transparent bees fly back into the story and into Barnaby's hives and the transparent, hybrid flower inside you begins to grow. Higher and higher and higher it grows, towards the sun that hovers inside you, the sun that hovers high above the transparent flower.

Higher and higher and higher, the transparent flower grows, getting closer and closer and closer to the shining sun.

Now the transparent flower *reaches* the sun and becomes one with it, so that where once was a transparent flower and a shining sun, there is now a shining flower. The shining flower removes its shining roots from you, dear readers, and it bends its shining stem into a circle and it pierces each of its shining petals with each of its shining roots. And in the story, Barnaby smiles.

Everything Was Strange

Everything was strange.

I remember a big ball of flames spinning fast in black. No, that can't be right, surely. But yes, I remember it. A big ball of flames spinning fast in black. In fact, now I think of it, there were billions of them. Billions of balls of flames spinning fast in black. And I was in the middle of them, standing on a spinning ball of rock, selling xylophones.

It was all so very strange.

Sometimes I'd become so engrossed in the particulars of xylophone selling that I would forget about the strangeness of it all and just get on with it. Then suddenly I'd remember: I am standing on a spinning ball of rock surrounded by billions of balls of flames spinning fast in black.

So very strange.

Why was it the way that it was? Why was it one way and not another? There may as well have been billions of xylophones spinning fast in black, with me in the middle of them, standing on a spinning ball of rock, selling balls of flames. That would have been no less strange. Eventually I'd have become engrossed in the particulars of balls of flames selling and forgotten about the strangeness of it all.

My life appeared strange because it was one way and not another. Only if it had been every possibility at once would it have not appeared strange. And that is what I am now: every possibility at once. And nothing is strange.

www.strangebooks.com

If you enjoyed this book, please spread the strangeness
by telling your friends. Plus, visit our website and sign
up to be notified of new publications, offers and
merchandise. Best wishes to you,

Mike Russell

Made in the USA
Middletown, DE
12 November 2019